CLASSICS ILLUSTRATED™

presents

ALL QUIET ON THE WESTERN FRONT

by Erich Maria Remarque

VINTAGE REPLICA EDITION

CLASSICS ILLUSTRATED: ALL QUIET ON THE WESTERN FRONT
ISBN: 9781911238232

Published by CCS Books
A trading name of Classic Comic Store Ltd.
Unit B, Castle Industrial Park, Pear Tree Lane, Newbury, Berkshire, RG14 2EZ, UK

Email: enquiries@ccsbooks.com
Tel: UK 01635 30890

This edition first published: 2019

Painted cover: Maurice del Bourgo
Illustrated by: Maurice del Bourgo
Adaptation: Kenneth W. Fitch
Re-origination: Shane Kirshenblatt
Additional material: A. J. Scopino and Jon Brooks

Printed in Turkey

ALL QUIET ON THE WESTERN FRONT

by Erich Maria Remarque

THIS BOOK IS TO BE NEITHER AN ACCUSATION NOR A CONFESSION, AND LEAST OF ALL AN ADVENTURE, FOR DEATH IS NOT AN ADVENTURE TO THOSE WHO STAND FACE TO FACE WITH IT. IT WILL TRY SIMPLY TO TELL OF A GENERATION OF MEN WHO, EVEN THOUGH THEY MAY HAVE ESCAPED ITS SHELLS, WERE DESTROYED BY THE WAR.

Erich Maria Remarque

Illustrated By
Maurice Del Bourgo

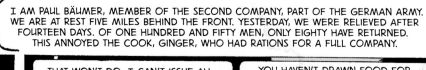

I AM PAUL BÄUMER, MEMBER OF THE SECOND COMPANY, PART OF THE GERMAN ARMY. WE ARE AT REST FIVE MILES BEHIND THE FRONT. YESTERDAY, WE WERE RELIEVED AFTER FOURTEEN DAYS. OF ONE HUNDRED AND FIFTY MEN, ONLY EIGHTY HAVE RETURNED. THIS ANNOYED THE COOK, GINGER, WHO HAD RATIONS FOR A FULL COMPANY.

THAT WON'T DO. I CAN'T ISSUE ALL THOSE RATIONS FOR ONLY EIGHTY MEN.

YOU HAVEN'T DRAWN FOOD FOR EIGHTY MEN. YOU'VE DRAWN IT FOR THE SECOND COMPANY. GOOD. LET'S HAVE IT THEN. WE *ARE* THE SECOND COMPANY!

FOR A WHILE, THINGS LOOKED BAD FOR GINGER, BUT OUR COMPANY COMMANDER, A LIEUTENANT, APPEARED IN TIME...

SERVE UP THE WHOLE ISSUE. AND BRING ME A PLATEFUL, TOO.

NOW WE WERE SATISFIED AND AT PEACE. OUR BELLIES WERE FILLED WITH HARICOT BEANS, SAUSAGE AND BREAD. MOREOVER, THE MAIL HAD COME, AND ALMOST EVERY MAN HAD A COUPLE OF LETTERS...

KANTOREK SENDS YOU ALL HIS BEST WISHES.

I WISH HE WAS HERE.

KANTOREK HAD BEEN OUR SCHOOLMASTER. THOSE OF US WHO CAME STRAIGHT FROM SCHOOL TO THE ARMY REMEMBER KANTOREK ONLY TOO WELL. WE CAN RECALL HOW HE WOULD STRUT BEFORE US AND SAY, IN A MOVING VOICE...

COME, COME, COME, LADS! WON'T YOU JOIN UP? BÄUMER? MÜLLER? KROPP? LEER?

JOSEF BEHM WAS THE ONLY ONE OF US WHO DID NOT WANT TO FIGHT – THAT IS, HE HAD THE COURAGE TO SAY SO...

IF YOU WON'T TAKE UP ARMS, YOU ARE A COWARD! YOU LADS ARE THE HOPE OF THE FATHERLAND!

THERE ARE THOUSANDS OF KANTOREKS. THEY SHOULD HAVE BEEN ADVISORS TO US LADS OF EIGHTEEN. INSTEAD... WELL, BEHM WAS THE FIRST OF US TO FALL, – A BULLET IN THE EYE.

BUT TO GO BACK FURTHER, IT WAS AT BASIC TRAINING CAMP THAT WE MET CORPORAL HIMMELSTOSS...

SO YOU THINK YOU ARE SOLDIERS, EH? WELL, WE ARE GOING TO SEE! FORWARD MARCH!

WE SOON LEARNED THAT A BRIGHT BUTTON IS MORE IMPORTANT THAN BOOKS. WHAT MATTERS IS NOT THE MIND, BUT THE BOOT BRUSH; NOT INTELLIGENCE, BUT THE SYSTEM; NOT FREEDOM, BUT DRILL...

SQUAD'S RIGHT, MARCH!

HIMMELSTOSS HAD A SPECIAL DISLIKE FOR KROPP, TJADEN, WESTHUS AND ME, BECAUSE HE SENSED A QUIET DEFIANCE...

YOU FOUR NEED SPECIAL INSTRUCTION. YOU WILL FOLLOW ME!

WE WERE LED TO A PLOUGHED FIELD. IT HAD RAINED THE NIGHT BEFORE, AND THE FIELD WAS VERY MUDDY...

PREPARE TO ADVANCE!

LIE DOWN!

ATTENTION! PREPARE TO ADVANCE!

LIE DOWN!

TIME AFTER TIME, HIMMELSTOSS REPEATED THAT COMMAND, UNTIL WE WERE EXHAUSTED, SCARCELY ABLE TO RISE...

ATTENTION! SNAP INTO IT! WHAT'S THE MATTER WITH YOU?

YOU WILL APPEAR BEFORE ME AT CAMP WITHIN FOUR HOURS. SEE THAT THERE IS NOT A SPOT OF DIRT ON YOU! DISMISSED!

SOMEDAY, WE WILL GET OUR REVENGE. A MAN CAN'T BE AS MEAN AS HIMMELSTOSS AND NOT PAY FOR IT!

HE WAS A POSTMAN IN CIVILIAN LIFE, TJADEN. HE'S DRUNK WITH HIS OWN SENSE OF IMPORTANCE NOW.

LATER...

DO YOU THINK THIS IS A CLEAN UNIFORM, BÄUMER? LOOK THERE! A SPOT OF DIRT! THIS WON'T DO, BÄUMER!

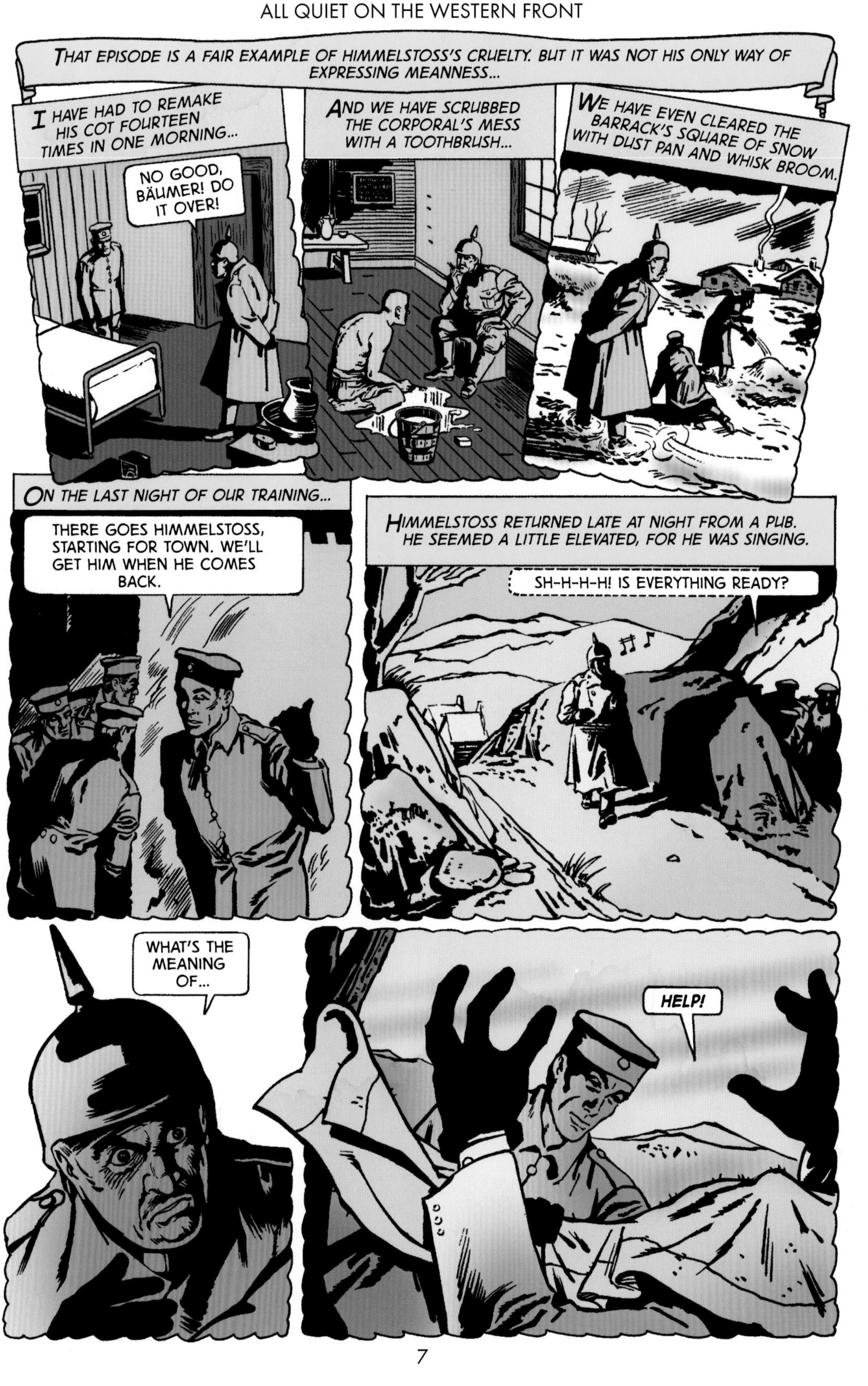
THAT EPISODE IS A FAIR EXAMPLE OF HIMMELSTOSS'S CRUELTY. BUT IT WAS NOT HIS ONLY WAY OF EXPRESSING MEANNESS...
I HAVE HAD TO REMAKE HIS COT FOURTEEN TIMES IN ONE MORNING...
NO GOOD, BÄUMER! DO IT OVER!
AND WE HAVE SCRUBBED THE CORPORAL'S MESS WITH A TOOTHBRUSH...
WE HAVE EVEN CLEARED THE BARRACK'S SQUARE OF SNOW WITH DUST PAN AND WHISK BROOM.
ON THE LAST NIGHT OF OUR TRAINING...
THERE GOES HIMMELSTOSS, STARTING FOR TOWN. WE'LL GET HIM WHEN HE COMES BACK.
HIMMELSTOSS RETURNED LATE AT NIGHT FROM A PUB. HE SEEMED A LITTLE ELEVATED, FOR HE WAS SINGING.
SH-H-H-H! IS EVERYTHING READY?
WHAT'S THE MEANING OF...
HELP!

I'LL GET YOU A COURT-MARTIAL! **OUCH!**

OKAY... PULL!

IT WAS A WONDERFUL PICTURE...

HIMMELSTOSS NEVER DISCOVERED WHOM HE HAD TO THANK. WE LEFT THE NEXT MORNING...

WHAT DO YOU SUPPOSE HIMMELSTOSS IS DOING NOW, HAIE?

PROBABLY TRYING TO REQUISITION A NEW PAIR OF TROUSERS!

IN SPITE OF EVERYTHING, WE HAD MUCH REASON TO THANK HIMMELSTOSS. BECAUSE OF HIM, WE BECAME HARD, SUSPICIOUS, PITILESS, VICIOUS, TOUGH – AND THAT WAS GOOD. HAD WE HAD GONE INTO THE TRENCHES WITHOUT THIS PERIOD OF TRAINING, MOST OF US WOULD CERTAINLY HAVE GONE MAD. ONLY THUS WERE WE PREPARED FOR WHAT AWAITED US. BUT BY FAR THE MOST IMPORTANT WAS THAT IT AWAKENED IN US A STRONG, PRACTICAL SENSE OF ESPRIT DE CORPS, WHICH IN THE FIELD DEVELOPED INTO THE FINEST THING THAT AROSE OUT OF THE WAR... COMRADESHIP.

IT WAS EASY TO UNDERSTAND OUR ATTITUDE TOWARDS THE FACTS MENTIONED IN THE LETTER FROM KANTOREK. BUT THERE WAS OTHER BUSINESS TO ATTEND TO...

THESE THINGS BELONG TO KEMMERICH. WE'LL TAKE THEM WHEN WE GO TO SEE HIM.

THREE OF US FORMER STUDENTS, MÜLLER, KROPP, AND I, WENT TO THE DRESSING STATION. FRANZ KEMMERICH, ALSO A FORMER STUDENT WHO HAD BEEN WOUNDED, WAS GLAD TO SEE US, BUT HE WAS GREATLY WORRIED...

SOMEONE HAS STOLEN MY WATCH, AND I HAVE SUCH A PAIN IN MY FOOT.

I ALWAYS TOLD YOU THAT YOU SHOULD NOT CARRY SUCH A GOOD WATCH, FRANZ. AND AS FOR...

DON'T TELL HIM HE HAS LOST HIS LEG. HE'LL KNOW SOON ENOUGH.

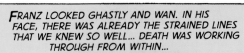

FRANZ LOOKED GHASTLY AND WAN. IN HIS FACE, THERE WAS ALREADY THE STRAINED LINES THAT WE KNEW SO WELL... DEATH WAS WORKING THROUGH FROM WITHIN...

WE HAVE BROUGHT YOUR THINGS, FRANZ.

PUT THEM UNDER THE BED.

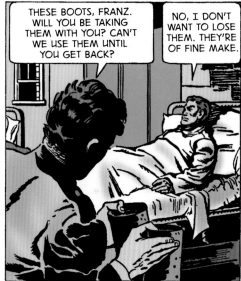

THESE BOOTS, FRANZ. WILL YOU BE TAKING THEM WITH YOU? CAN'T WE USE THEM UNTIL YOU GET BACK?

NO, I DON'T WANT TO LOSE THEM. THEY'RE OF FINE MAKE.

I TROD ON MÜLLER'S FOOT. RELUCTANTLY, HE PUT THE FINE BOOTS BACK UNDER THE BED. KEMMERICH GROANED. HE WAS FEVERISH...

WAIT, FRANZ. ALBERT AND I WILL TRY TO GET SOMETHING FOR THAT PAIN IN YOUR FOOT.

OUR FRIEND, KEMMERICH, IS IN BAD SHAPE AND IN GREAT PAIN. CAN'T YOU GIVE A DOSE OF MORPHIA?

IT'S IMPOSSIBLE. IF WE WERE TO GIVE MORPHIA TO EVERYONE, WE WOULD HAVE TO HAVE TUBS FULL.

YOU ONLY ATTEND TO THE OFFICERS PROPERLY!

WAIT, ALBERT, WAIT!

I REALISED ALBERT WAS GETTING NOWHERE. I HAD EXTRA CIGARETTES FROM OUR DOUBLE RATIONS. I PRESSED THEM INTO THE ORDERLY'S HAND...

COULDN'T YOU DO US A FAVOUR? FRANZ KEMMERICH IS IN VERY GREAT PAIN.

WELL... ALL RIGHT...

*W*E WENT BACK TO THE HUTS. I THOUGHT OF THE LETTER I MUST WRITE TO KEMMERICH'S MOTHER. I THOUGHT OF FRANZ, WHO, A LITTLE WHILE AGO, WAS ROASTING HORSE-FLESH WITH US AND HUDDLING IN SHELL HOLES...

IF FRANZ PASSES OUT IN THE NIGHT, THOSE ORDERLIES WILL TAKE THE BOOTS.

THE DIRTY SWINE!

*K*ROPP SAW RED EVERY ONCE IN A WHILE. WE TALKED TO CALM HIM DOWN...

WHAT ELSE DID KANTOREK WRITE TO YOU, ALBERT?

HE WRITES: "YOU ARE THE IRON YOUTH!" THAT'S HOW THEY THINK, THOSE THOUSANDS OF KANTOREKS! IRON YOUTH! WE ARE NONE OF US MORE THAN TWENTY, YET WE ARE OLD!

*T*HE NEXT DAY, I WENT ALONE TO SEE KEMMERICH...

I KNOW NOW, PAUL. TAKE MY BOOTS FOR MÜLLER... IF YOU FIND MY WATCH, SEND IT HOME. AND WILL YOU WRITE TO MY MOTHER?

DON'T TALK LIKE THAT, FRANZ. JUST REST UP AND EAT YOUR FOOD AND YOU WILL SOON BE WELL AGAIN.

*S*UDDENLY, KEMMERICH GROANED AND BEGAN TO GURGLE. I RUSHED FOR THE DOCTOR... THE DOCTOR SAID: "IF HE'S DYING, I CAN'T HELP HIM. I HAVE AMPUTATED FIVE LEGS TODAY. LET AN ORDERLY TAKE CARE OF THE MATTER"... WHEN WE REACHED FRANZ, HE WAS DEAD...

ARE YOU TAKING HIS THINGS? WE MUST GET HIM AWAY AT ONCE.

YES, I'LL TAKE THEM.

*O*UTSIDE, I WAS AWARE OF THE DARKNESS, AND THE WIND WAS A DELIVERANCE. I BREATHED AS DEEP AS I COULD, AND FELT THE BREEZE IN MY FACE, WARM AND SOFT AS NEVER BEFORE. SOON, I REACHED MÜLLER'S HUT. HE WAITED FOR ME AND THE BOOTS.

SOMETIME LATER, WE HAD TO GO ON WIRING FATIGUE. THE MOTOR LORRIES ROLLED UP AFTER DARK...

I GUESS THIS ONE IS OURS, KAT.

IT MIGHT AS WELL BE THIS ONE AS ANY OTHER.

THE ENGINES DRONED; THE LORRIES BUMPED AND RATTLED. THE ROADS WERE FULL OF HOLES...

NO GUARANTEE YOU WON'T BE THROWN OUT OF HERE, KAT.

ARE YOU WORRIED, PAUL? AFTER ALL, A BROKEN ARM IS BETTER THAN A HOLE IN THE BELLY.

SUDDENLY, I HEARD DISTINCTLY THE CACKLE OF GEESE...

KAT, I HEAR SOME ASPIRANTS FOR THE FRYING PAN OVER THERE!

IT WILL BE ATTENDED TO WHEN WE COME BACK. I HAVE THEIR NUMBER.

OF COURSE, KAT HAD THEIR NUMBER. HE KNEW ALL ABOUT EVERY LEG OF GOOSE WITHIN A FIFTEEN-MILE RADIUS. KAT, WHOSE FULL NAME WAS STANISLAUS KATCZINSKY, WAS A COBBLER, BUT HE UNDERSTOOD ALL TRADES. HE HAD A NOSE FOR DIRTY WEATHER, GOOD FOOD, AND SOFT JOBS.

THE LORRIES ARRIVED AT THE ARTILLERY LINE. THE GUN EMPLACEMENTS WERE CAMOUFLAGED. THE AIR BECAME ACRID WITH THE SMOKE OF GUNS. THE FUMES OF POWDER TASTED BITTER ON THE TONGUE.

THE NEW RECRUITS ARE NERVOUS. THEY DON'T KNOW WHY, BUT I CAN TELL YOU. THERE'LL BE A BOMBARDMENT. I CAN FEEL IT IN MY BONES.

SOON, SHELLS LANDED AND EXPLODED NEAR US. BUT EVEN BEFORE THEY HIT, WE WERE ON THE GROUND, SO THAT FRAGMENTS WHISTLED ABOVE US. ONE CANNOT EXPLAIN IT. WE WERE PROTECTED, IT SEEMS, BY OUR ANIMAL INSTINCT...

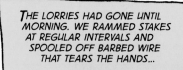

THE LORRIES HAD GONE UNTIL MORNING. WE RAMMED STAKES AT REGULAR INTERVALS AND SPOOLED OFF BARBED WIRE THAT TEARS THE HANDS...

I WISH WE WERE BACK AT THE HUTS. I DON'T LIKE THIS TONIGHT.

AFTER A FEW HOURS, IT WAS DONE. MOST OF US LAY DOWN AND SLEPT UNTIL THE LORRIES CAME. I AWOKE SUDDENLY. I WAS GLAD KAT WAS HERE, SMOKING HIS PIPE WITH THE COVERED BOWL...

THAT GAVE YOU A FRIGHT. IT WAS ONLY A NOSECAP. IT LANDED IN THE BUSHES OVER THERE. MIGHTY FINE FIREWORKS, IF THEY WERE NOT SO DANGEROUS!

THEN IT BEGAN IN EARNEST...

I TOLD YOU THERE WOULD BE A BOMBARD-MENT!

YOU WERE SO RIGHT!

I FOUND A RECRUIT IN UTTER TERROR...

LOOK, SON, FLATTEN DOWN AND PUT ON YOUR HELMET!

HE PUSHED THE HELMET OFF, AND LIKE A CHILD, CREPT UNDER MY ARM. THE LITTLE SHOULDERS HEAVED, SHOULDERS JUST LIKE KEMMERICH'S...

AT LAST, IT GREW QUIET...

ALL OVER, KID. IT'S ALL RIGHT THIS TIME.

IT GOT SOME PRETTY BADLY. CRIES WERE HEARD. BUT ALBERT SAID...

LISTEN! THAT'S NOT MEN SCREAMING!

WHAT IS IT, THEN?

IT'S WOUNDED HORSES.

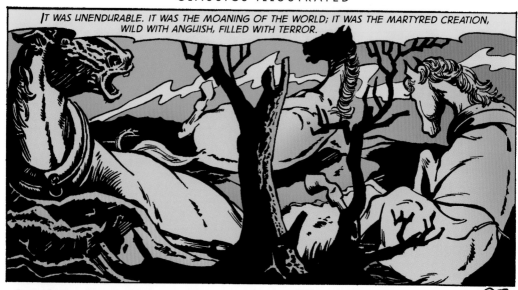

IT WAS UNENDURABLE. IT WAS THE MOANING OF THE WORLD; IT WAS THE MARTYRED CREATION, WILD WITH ANGUISH, FILLED WITH TERROR.

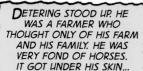

DETERING STOOD UP. HE WAS A FARMER WHO THOUGHT ONLY OF HIS FARM AND HIS FAMILY. HE WAS VERY FOND OF HORSES. IT GOT UNDER HIS SKIN...

WHY DON'T THEY SHOOT THEM?

IT'S THE VILEST BASENESS TO BRING HORSES INTO WAR! WHAT HARM HAVE THEY DONE?

ARE YOU MAD? THE HORSES MUST WAIT! YOU MAY KILL SOME OF OUR MEN!

WE SAT DOWN AND HELD OUR EARS. BUT THAT APPALLING NOISE, THOSE GROANS AND SCREAMS, THEY PENETRATED EVERYWHERE...

WE TRIED TO TELL OURSELVES THAT THIS WAS WAR, BUT IT WAS NO GOOD. THEN, SINGLE SHOTS CRACKED OUT. WE TOOK OUR HANDS FROM OUR EARS. THE CRIES WERE SILENCED. ONLY A LONG-DRAWN DYING SIGH HUNG ON THE AIR...

WE WENT BACK. IT WAS THREE O' CLOCK – TIME TO RETURN TO THE LORRIES...

IT'S ABOUT OVER, KAT.

I DON'T KNOW, PAUL. I DON'T KNOW...

TAKE COVER! IT'S COMING AGAIN!

THE BOMBARDMENT WAS ON AGAIN. THERE WAS NO PLACE TO TAKE COVER, EXCEPT BEHIND THE GRAVEYARD MOUNDS.

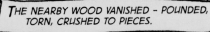

THE NEARBY WOOD VANISHED – POUNDED, TORN, CRUSHED TO PIECES.

THE DARK WENT MAD. IT HEAVED AND RAVED. THEN, FLAMES AND EXPLOSIONS BANISHED THE DARKNESS AND REPLACED IT WITH HORROR...

A HOLE WAS TORN OUT IN FRONT OF ME. WITH ONE BOUND, I FLUNG MYSELF TOWARDS IT, FOR SHELLS HARDLY EVER LANDED IN THE SAME HOLE TWICE.

I DROPPED ON THE GROUND, FLAT AS A FISH. THE EARTH LEAPED, THE BLAST THUNDERED IN MY EARS. A HAND BRUSHED MY FACE...

I OPENED MY EYES – MY FINGERS GRASPED A SLEEVE, AN ARM. A WOUNDED MAN? I YELLED TO HIM – NO ANSWER – A DEAD MAN. MY HAND GROPED FURTHER, SPLINTERS OF WOOD – NOW I REMEMBERED AGAIN THAT WE WERE LYING IN THE GRAVEYARD.

THE SHELLING WAS HEAVIER THAN EVER...

IT WIPED OUT THE SENSIBILITIES... I CRAWLED INTO THE COFFIN FOR PROTECTION...

PAUL! PAUL!

16

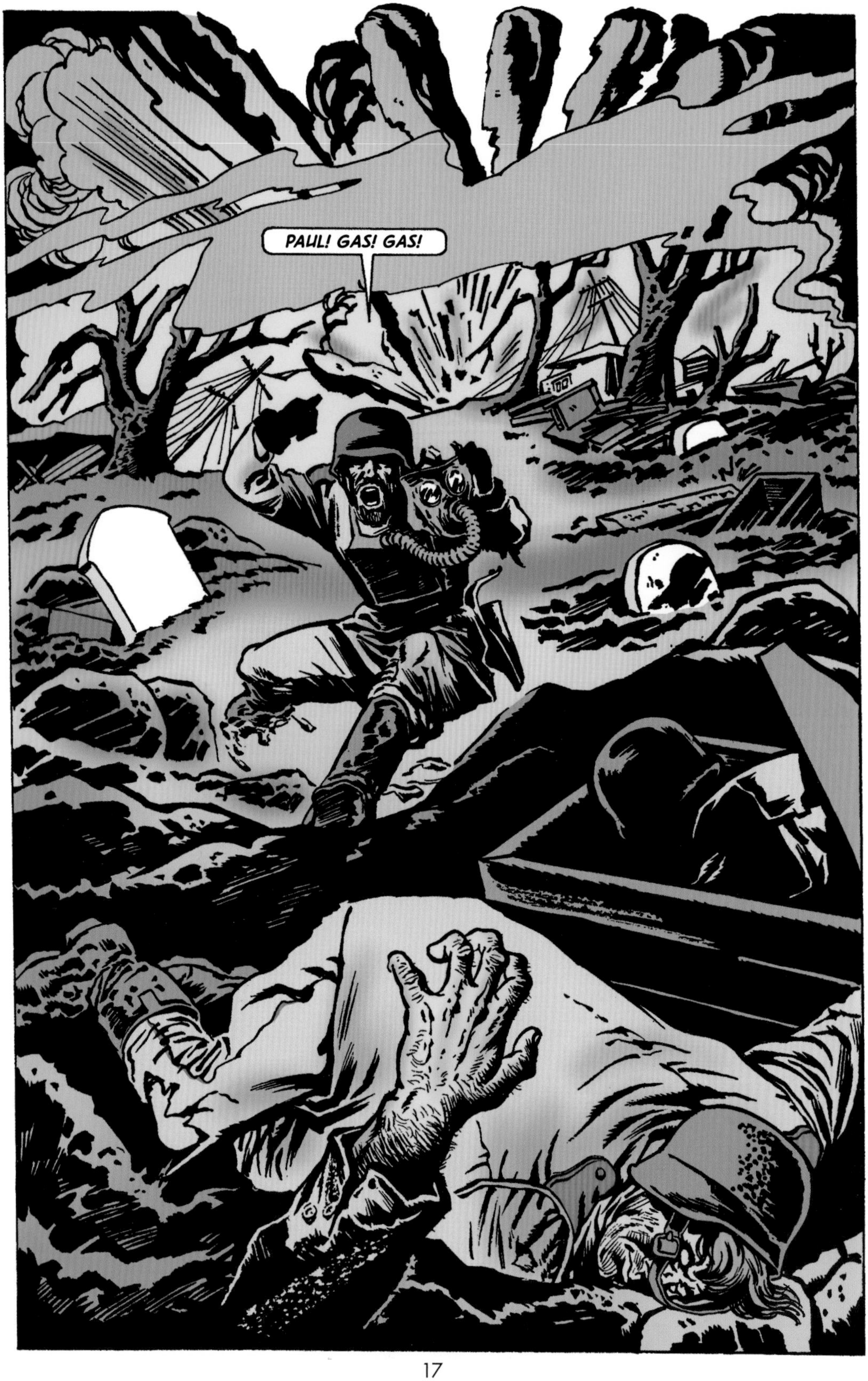
PAUL! GAS! GAS!

GAS! GAS! GAAAS! PASS IT ON!

I GRABBED FOR MY GAS MASK. I EMERGED FROM THE SHELL HOLE, FOR THE POISONOUS FUMES STAY THERE LONGEST. SOME DISTANCE FROM ME LIES SOMEONE. I THINK OF NOTHING BUT THAT HE MUST KNOW...

GAS! GAAAS!

I LAY FLAT ON THE GROUND, TRUSTING THAT THERE WERE NO LEAKS IN MY MASK. SOON MY HEAD BOOMED AND ROARED, AND MY LUNGS WERE TIGHT. THE GAS, LIKE A BIG SOFT JELLYFISH, LOLLED OBSCENELY ABOUT US...

THE SHELLING HAD STOPPED. I PEERED THROUGH MY FOGGED-UP WINDOWS. I SAW A MAN WITHOUT HIS MASK. I TORE MY MASK OFF, TOO, AND STUMBLED FORWARDS AS THE AIR STREAMED INTO ME LIKE COLD WATER...

I KICKED SOMEONE...

I'M SORRY, I DIDN'T SEE YOU.

I KNELT DOWN. HE WAS ONLY A BOY. I RECOGNISED HIM – THE RECRUIT WHO HAD BEEN SO FRIGHTENED...

WHERE HAS IT GOT YOU, COMRADE?

HELP ME WITH THE KID. HE'S IN BAD SHAPE.

LET'S LOOK AT THE WOUND.

THE WHOLE HIP IS ONE MASS OF MINCEMEAT AND BONE SPLINTERS. THE KID'LL NEVER WALK AGAIN.

KAT HAD SPREAD OUT TWO WADS OF DRESSING AS WIDE AS POSSIBLE, AND HAD BOUND THE WOUNDS LOOSELY. IT WAS ALL HE COULD DO...

HE'LL LIVE THREE OR FOUR DAYS. SHOULDN'T WE JUST PUT AN END TO IT?

YES, KAT. PUT HIM OUT OF HIS MISERY.

KAT HAD MADE UP HIS MIND. WE LOOKED AROUND. BUT WE WERE NO LONGER ALONE. A SMALL GROUP WAS APPROACHING FROM THE SHELL HOLE.

WE CAN'T DO IT NOW. BETTER GET HIM A STRETCHER. SUCH A KID. SUCH A LITTLE KID...

NOW HE IS NUMB AND FEELS NOTHING. IN AN HOUR HE WILL BE ONE SCREAMING BUNDLE OF INTOLERABLE PAIN.

MONOTONOUSLY THE LORRIES SWAYED. MONOTONOUSLY RAIN FELL – ON OUR HEADS, ON THE HEADS OF THE DEAD, ON THE BODY OF THE LITTLE RECRUIT, ON KEMMERICH'S GRAVE. AND IT FELL IN OUR HEARTS.

19

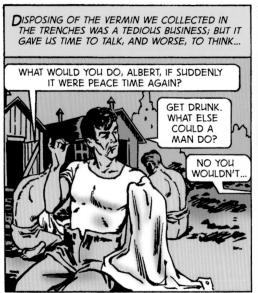

DISPOSING OF THE VERMIN WE COLLECTED IN THE TRENCHES WAS A TEDIOUS BUSINESS; BUT IT GAVE US TIME TO TALK, AND WORSE, TO THINK...

WHAT WOULD YOU DO, ALBERT, IF SUDDENLY IT WERE PEACE TIME AGAIN?

GET DRUNK. WHAT ELSE COULD A MAN DO?

NO YOU WOULDN'T...

YOU'D GO HOME, JUST AS I WOULD. LOOK, MY OLD PEOPLE.

IT'S ALRIGHT FOR YOU TO TALK, KAT. YOU HAVE A WIFE AND CHILDREN...

NEVER MIND WHAT WE WOULD DO IN PEACE. LOOK WHO IS COMING. HIMMELSTOSS! WHAT WILL WE DO NOW?

WELL? I SEE YOU ARE ALL HERE, TOO.

A BIT LONGER THAN YOU, I FANCY.

WHAT? I GUESS YOU DON'T REMEMBER ME!

OH, YES WE DO! AND DO YOU KNOW WHAT WE THINK YOU ARE? A DIRTY HOUND!

SINCE WHEN HAVE WE BECOME SO FAMILIAR? I DON'T REMEMBER THAT WE EVER SLEPT IN THE GUTTER TOGETHER?

NO, YOU SLEPT THERE YOURSELF!

BY NOW, HIMMELSTOSS WAS A RAGING BOOK OF ARMY REGULATIONS...

TJADEN, I COMMAND YOU AS YOUR SUPERIOR OFFICER: STAND UP!

YOU'RE AT THE FRONT NOW, HIMMELSTOSS. AND YOU KNOW WHAT YOU CAN DO!

THE RESULT OF THE INSUBORDINATION WAS THREE DAYS' OPEN ARREST FOR TJADEN AND ONE DAY FOR KROPP. OPEN ARREST WAS QUITE PLEASANT. THE CLINK WAS ONCE A FOWL-HOUSE. THERE WE COULD VISIT THE PRISONERS. WE PLAYED SKAT FAR INTO THE NIGHT...

WELL, I'M BROKE. I'LL HAVE TO QUIT.

I'M WAY AHEAD, SO IT'S AS GOOD A TIME AS ANY.

AFTER WE BROKE UP, KAT SAID...

WHAT DO YOU SAY TO SOME ROAST GOOSE?

NOT BAD...

IT COST US TWO CIGARETTES TO RIDE OUT ON A MUNITIONS WAGON TO THE BARNYARD WE PASSED ON THE WAY TO WIRING FATIGUE...

COME. I'LL HOIST YOU OVER THE FENCE...

I WAITED A FEW MOMENTS, THEN, SOFTLY, I STOLE THROUGH THE DOOR. SUDDENLY, THERE WAS BEDLAM. WHAT A KICK A GOOSE HAS!

ARE YOU ALL RIGHT, PAUL?

DAYS BEFORE, KAT DISCOVERED A DESERTED SHACK NEARBY. WE CURTAINED THE LONE WINDOW AND MADE A FIRE IN THE STOVE. IT TOOK A LONG WHILE TO ROAST A GOOSE, BUT FINALLY...

IT'S DONE!

KAT, I LOVE YOU!

THE SOUND OF GUNFIRE PENETRATED OUR REFUGE. SOMETIMES A HEAVY CRASH AND THE SHACK SHIVERED. WE WERE TWO MINUTE SPARKS OF LIFE; OUTSIDE WAS A CIRCLE OF DEATH. NOW WE SAT WITH THE GOOSE BETWEEN US AND DID NOT EVEN SPEAK...

LATER, WE WOKE KROPP AND TJADEN...

I SWEAR YOU TWO ARE MAGICIANS!

I'M INCLINED TO AGREE WITH YOU!

MAY I NEVER FORGET YOU!

SEVERAL DAYS PASSED. THERE WERE RUMOURS OF AN OFFENSIVE. ON THE WAY TO THE FRONT, WE PASSED A SHELLED SCHOOLHOUSE, AND AGAINST IT A PILE OF BRAND NEW COFFINS...

THEY ARE FOR US. GOOD PREPARATION FOR AN OFFENSIVE.

BE THANKFUL IF YOU GET SO MUCH AS A COFFIN FOR YOUR CARCASS, DETERING!

THE ENGLISH ARTILLERY WAS STRENGTHENED. WE WERE IN LOW SPIRITS. THE FRONT WAS A CAGE IN WHICH WE AWAITED FEARFULLY WHATEVER MAY HAPPEN. WE LAY UNDER A NETWORK OF ARCHING SHELLS, AND TRUSTED TO LUCK...

HOW WILL IT BE, PAUL? WILL WE BE HERE TOMORROW?

IF IT COMES, ALL WE CAN DO IS DUCK.

SUDDENLY, A SHELL FELL IN THE TRENCH. MANY WERE KILLED, AND MORE WOUNDED...

IT WAS ONE OF OUR OWN SHELLS! THE BARRELS MUST BE WORN OUT!

IT GOT BAD...

WE'LL GET IN THE DUGOUT! THIS IS ONLY THE BEGINNING!

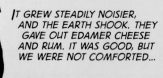

IT GREW STEADILY NOISIER, AND THE EARTH SHOOK. THEY GAVE OUT EDAMER CHEESE AND RUM. IT WAS GOOD, BUT WE WERE NOT COMFORTED...

THEY ALWAYS GIVE OUT CHEESE AND RUM WHEN A BAD TIME IS COMING.

IT WILL BE LIKE THE SOMME. WE WERE SHELLED STEADILY THERE FOR SEVEN DAYS AND NIGHTS.

WE WOKE IN THE MIDDLE OF THE NIGHT. EVERY MAN WAS AWARE OF THE HEAVY SHELLS. A FEW RECRUITS WERE GREEN AND SICK. THERE WOULD BE NO MORE SLEEP...

ONE OF THE RECRUITS WENT BERSERK...

WAIT A MINUTE! WHERE ARE YOU GOING!

LEAVE ME ALONE! I'LL BE BACK IN A MINUTE!

NO YOU DON'T! GRAB HIM, KAT!

THOUGH HE RAVED AND HIS EYES ROLLED, IT COULDN'T BE HELPED. WE HAD TO GIVE HIM A HIDING. WE DID IT QUICKLY AND MERCILESSLY. OTHERWISE, HE WOULD HAVE RUN STRAIGHT TO HIS DEATH...

SUDDENLY, THE NEARER EXPLOSIONS CEASED... WE WAITED, READY... PERHAPS IT WOULD BE GAS, PERHAPS ATTACK...

DAWN...

THIS IS IT, KAT!

WE SAW THE STORM-TROOPS COMING. OUR ARTILLERY OPENED FIRE. MACHINE-GUNS RATTLED, RIFLES CRACKED. WE RECOGNISED THE DISTORTED FACES... THE SMOOTH HELMETS: THEY WERE FRENCH.

THE FIRST WAVE OF ATTACK WAS REPULSED. WE ROSE TO MEET THE ENEMY. PERHAPS... IT WOULD END. PERHAPS... WE WOULD COME THROUGH...

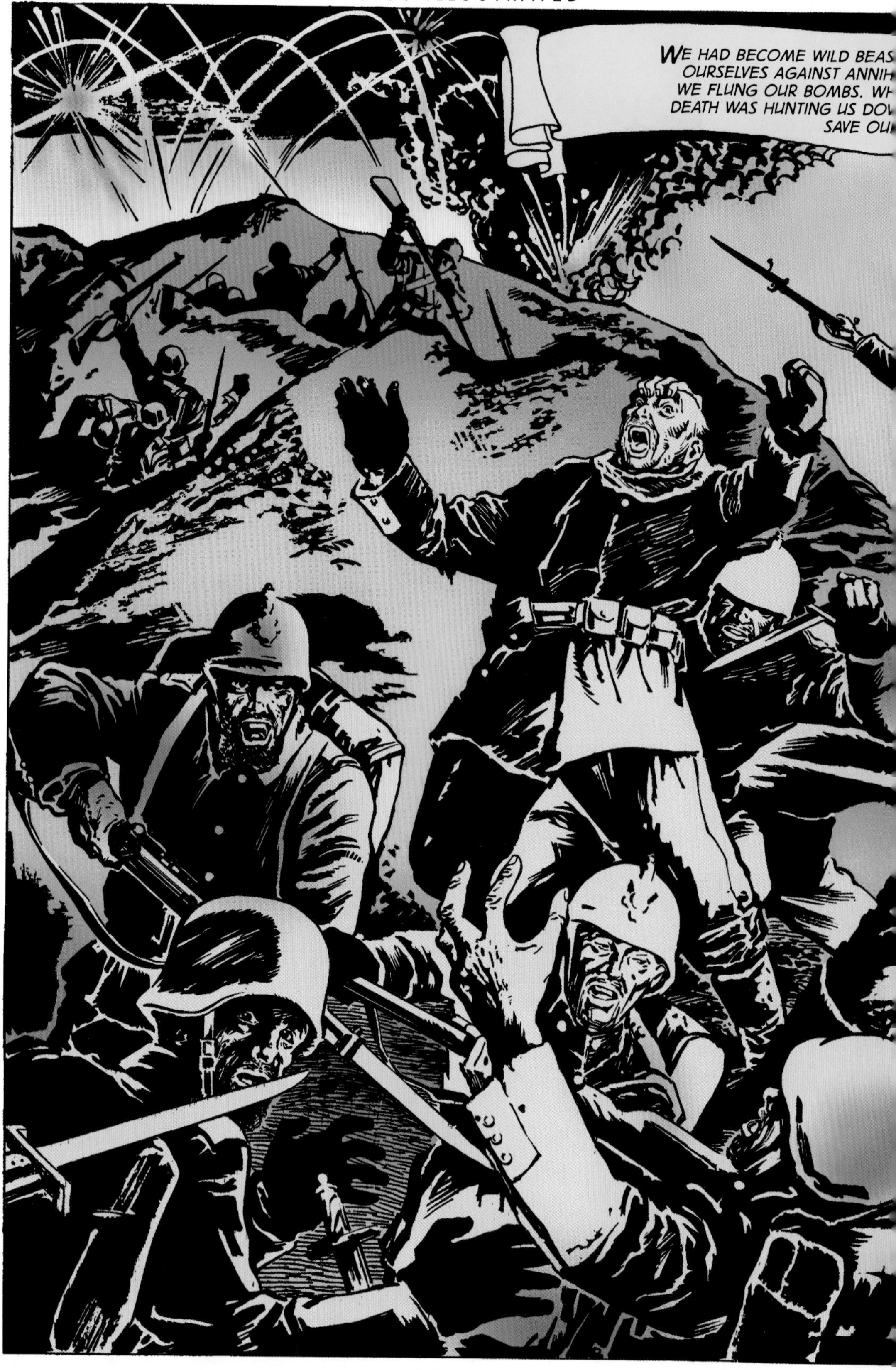
WE HAD BECOME WILD BEAS
OURSELVES AGAINST ANNIH
WE FLUNG OUR BOMBS. WH
DEATH WAS HUNTING US DOV
SAVE OU

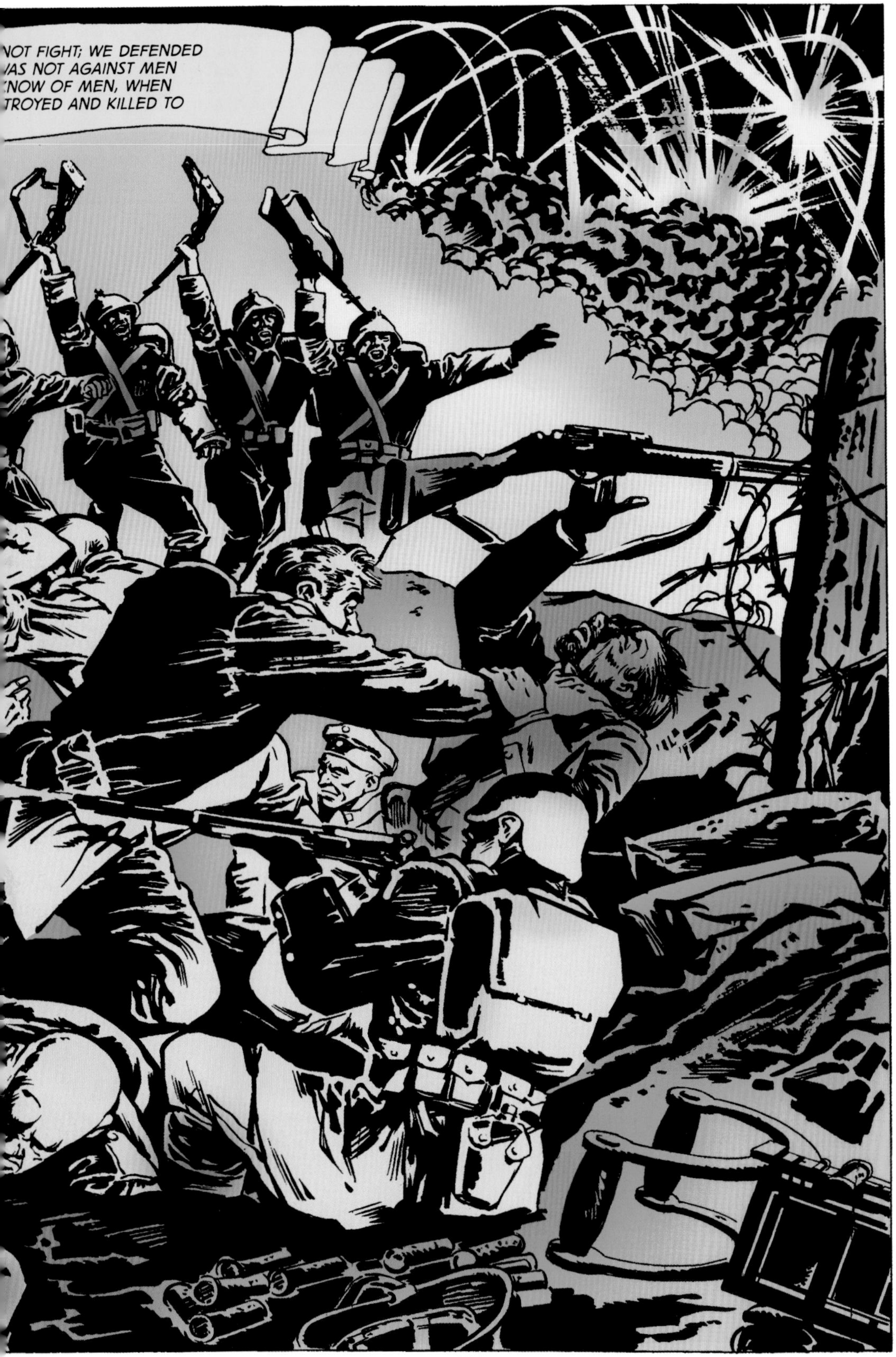
NOT FIGHT; WE DEFENDED
/AS NOT AGAINST MEN
NOW OF MEN, WHEN
TROYED AND KILLED TO

THE ATTACK HAD BEEN REPULSED. WE DROVE THE ENEMY BACK. WITH UTMOST HASTE, WE SEIZED WHATEVER PROVISIONS WE COULD FIND. WE WERE NOT GHOULS, BUT FOR ONCE KNEW WE WOULD HAVE SOMETHING GOOD TO EAT...

WE MADE OUR WAY BACK TO OUR POSITION. HAIE HAD SCORED A LOAF OF FRENCH BREAD; TJADEN TWO BOTTLES OF COGNAC. IT WENT WELL WITH THE TINS OF CORNED BEEF KAT AND I HAD BROUGHT...

MAYBE WE SHOULD TOAST THE FRENCHIES FOR THIS FEAST.

IT WAS CHILLY. I WAS ON SENTRY DUTY. AS ALWAYS, MY STRENGTH WAS EXHAUSTED AFTER AN ATTACK AND IT WAS HARD FOR ME TO BE ALONE WITH MY THOUGHTS...

THEY WERE NOT PROPERLY THOUGHTS: THEY WERE MEMORIES, WHICH IN MY WEAKNESS, TURNED HOMEWARD, AND I WAS A SCHOOLBOY WALKING BENEATH TALL POPLARS...

MY FLESH CREPT, AND YET THE NIGHT WAS WARM. BUT THE RATTLE OF MESS TINS BROUGHT ME BACK TO REALITY...

I'M GLAD MY STINT IS OVER; THAT YOU'RE GOING TO RELIEVE ME. I'M HUNGRY AFTER STANDING HERE SO LONG.

AND THEN, WITH THE GREY OF DAWN, ...COUNTER-ATTACK...

WE HAD TO KEEP THE ENEMY OFF BALANCE, – GIVE HIM NO CHANCE TO REGROUP HIS LINES...

ONLY A FOOL WOULD TRY TO STAND UP AGAINST THIS FIRE. OUR ARTILLERY WASN'T EFFECTIVE ENOUGH YET.

AND THEN, GAS!

I LAY WAITING FOR DEATH – OR LIFE – UNTIL I HEARD AN ORDER, AND KNEW THAT THE GAS HAD PASSED...

FORWARD... TO THE ATTACK!

HIMMELSTOSS! DIDN'T YOU HEAR THE ORDER?

I CAN'T! I'M WOUNDED!

I'LL BIND UP YOUR WOUND FOR YOU! LET'S SEE IT!

HIMMELSTOSS WAS UNWILLING TO LET ME SEE THE WOUND. I JERKED HIS ARM AND GRABBED HIM BY THE WRIST...

LET ME ALONE! I'M WOUNDED, I TELL YOU!

YOU LIAR! YOU COWARD! IT'S ONLY A SCRATCH!

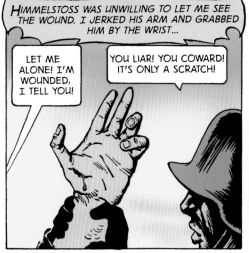

GET OUT! DO YOU HEAR? GET OUT!

YOU COW! YOU LUMP! YOU SWINE! GET UP!

NO!

ANOTHER WAVE OF OUR ATTACK HAD JUST COME UP. A LIEUTENANT WAS WITH THEM. HE SAW US AND YELLED...

COME ON, YOU TWO! JOIN IN! FOLLOW!

THE WORD OF COMMAND DID WHAT ALL MY BANGING COULD NOT. ONCE MORE HE WAS THE SMART HIMMELSTOSS OF THE PARADE GROUND...

MINES, TANKS, GUNS... WE SAW TIME PASS IN THE COLOURLESS FACES OF THE DYING. WE SHOT, WE KILLED. THE LITTLE PIECE OF CONVULSED EARTH WAS HELD. WE HAD YIELDED A FEW HUNDRED YARDS, BUT ON EVERY YARD THERE WAS A DEAD MAN...

I CRAWLED MISERABLY BACK TOWARDS THE TRENCH... AND THEN...

HAIE! HAIE! YOU'RE WOUNDED! LET ME HELP YOU!

DON'T BOTHER, PAUL! IT'S ALL UP! SAVE YOURSELF!

HAIE'S WHOLE BACK HAD BEEN SHATTERED. IF I MOVED HIM, HE WOULD DIE IN A MATTER OF MINUTES. I COULD ONLY PRESS HIS HAND AND CRAWL OUT...

I HAD A FURLOUGH. I HAD BIDDEN GOODBYE TO MY FRIENDS. MY TRAIN HAD PASSED FIELDS AND FARMYARDS. I HAD WALKED THROUGH THE TOWN FROM THE STATION AND I SAW OLD SCENES I HAD FORGOTTEN. NOW I WAS HOME...

THE STAIRS CREAKED UNDER MY BOOTS. UPSTAIRS A DOOR RATTLED. I SAW MY SISTER, ERNA...

PAUL! PAUL!

MY SISTER RAN TOWARDS MY MOTHER'S BEDROOM. I TRIED TO SPEAK, BUT NO WORDS CAME. AGAINST MY WILL TEARS RAN DOWN MY CHEEKS...

MOTHER! MOTHER! PAUL IS HERE!

HERE I AM, MOTHER.

ARE YOU WOUNDED?

WE WERE NOT A DEMONSTRATIVE FAMILY, BUT OUR WORDS HAD A DEEP MEANING TO ONE ANOTHER. MY MOTHER WAS VERY ILL, BUT HER ANXIETY WAS ALL FOR ME...

THEY SAY IT IS TERRIBLE. WITH THE GAS, AND SHELLS,... AND HARDSHIP.

THAT IS JUST TALK, MOTHER. THEY TAKE VERY GOOD CARE OF US. SEE, I AM WELL AND FIT.

I RECOVERED MY COMPOSURE AND ANSWERED MY MOTHER'S QUESTIONS CALMLY AND QUIETED HER FEARS, BUT AS SOON AS POSSIBLE, I SPOKE ALONE WITH MY SISTER...

WHAT IS THE MATTER WITH MOTHER?

THE DOCTORS SAY IT IS PROBABLY CANCER. WE DID NOT WRITE ABOUT IT, FOR WE DID NOT WANT TO WORRY YOU.

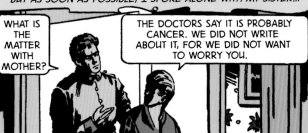

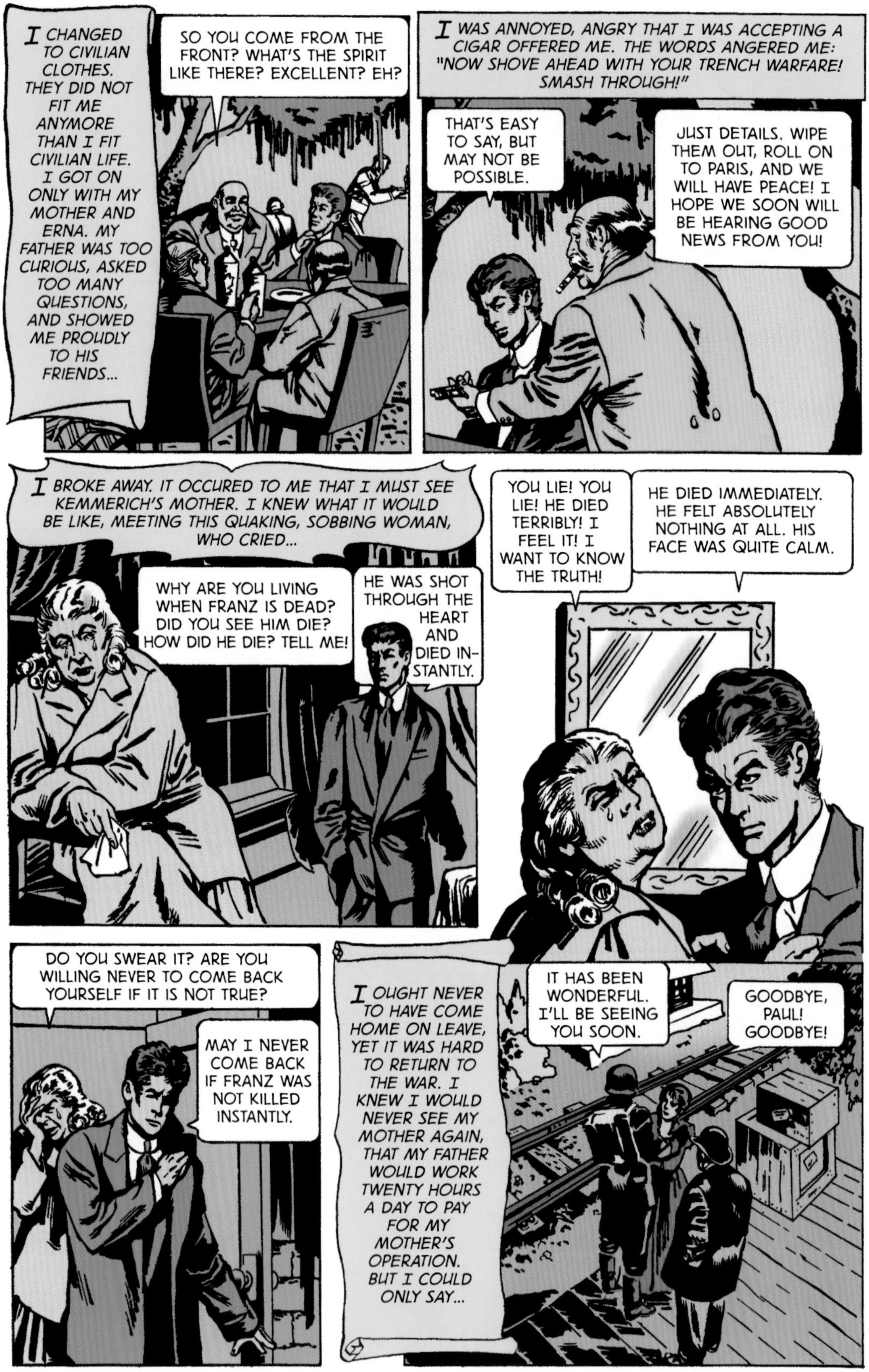
I CHANGED TO CIVILIAN CLOTHES. THEY DID NOT FIT ME ANYMORE THAN I FIT CIVILIAN LIFE. I GOT ON ONLY WITH MY MOTHER AND ERNA. MY FATHER WAS TOO CURIOUS, ASKED TOO MANY QUESTIONS, AND SHOWED ME PROUDLY TO HIS FRIENDS...
SO YOU COME FROM THE FRONT? WHAT'S THE SPIRIT LIKE THERE? EXCELLENT? EH?
I WAS ANNOYED, ANGRY THAT I WAS ACCEPTING A CIGAR OFFERED ME. THE WORDS ANGERED ME: "NOW SHOVE AHEAD WITH YOUR TRENCH WARFARE! SMASH THROUGH!"
THAT'S EASY TO SAY, BUT MAY NOT BE POSSIBLE.
JUST DETAILS. WIPE THEM OUT, ROLL ON TO PARIS, AND WE WILL HAVE PEACE! I HOPE WE SOON WILL BE HEARING GOOD NEWS FROM YOU!
I BROKE AWAY. IT OCCURED TO ME THAT I MUST SEE KEMMERICH'S MOTHER. I KNEW WHAT IT WOULD BE LIKE, MEETING THIS QUAKING, SOBBING WOMAN, WHO CRIED...
WHY ARE YOU LIVING WHEN FRANZ IS DEAD? DID YOU SEE HIM DIE? HOW DID HE DIE? TELL ME!
HE WAS SHOT THROUGH THE HEART AND DIED INSTANTLY.
YOU LIE! YOU LIE! HE DIED TERRIBLY! I FEEL IT! I WANT TO KNOW THE TRUTH!
HE DIED IMMEDIATELY. HE FELT ABSOLUTELY NOTHING AT ALL. HIS FACE WAS QUITE CALM.
DO YOU SWEAR IT? ARE YOU WILLING NEVER TO COME BACK YOURSELF IF IT IS NOT TRUE?
MAY I NEVER COME BACK IF FRANZ WAS NOT KILLED INSTANTLY.
I OUGHT NEVER TO HAVE COME HOME ON LEAVE, YET IT WAS HARD TO RETURN TO THE WAR. I KNEW I WOULD NEVER SEE MY MOTHER AGAIN, THAT MY FATHER WOULD WORK TWENTY HOURS A DAY TO PAY FOR MY MOTHER'S OPERATION. BUT I COULD ONLY SAY...
IT HAS BEEN WONDERFUL. I'LL BE SEEING YOU SOON.
GOODBYE, PAUL! GOODBYE!

AT THE BARRACKS, I WAS DETAINED FOR TWO DAYS, UNTIL MY COMPANY RETURNED FROM THE FIGHTING. I COULD SCARCELY CONTAIN MYSELF FOR JOY AT SEEING THEM ALL COME BACK SAFELY. THIS WAS WHERE I BELONGED...

YES, KAT, THE POTATO CAKES AND JAM ARE FROM MY MOTHER.

GOOD. I CAN TELL BY THE TASTE.

WE WERE AT THE FRONT. A PATROL HAD TO BE SENT OUT TO LEARN THE ENEMY'S POSITION. I VOLUNTEERED TO GO ALONE...

WE OUGHT TO SLIP THROUGH THE WIRE AND CREEP FORWARDS SEPARATELY. THERE'S PLENTY OF MACHINE-GUN FIRE.

I HAD BEEN AWAY TOO LONG. I WAS TERRIFIED AT FINDING MYSELF ALONE. I HAD TO PULL MYSELF TOGETHER. THIS WASN'T MY FIRST PATROL. IT WASN'T EVEN A VERY RISKY ONE.

I CRAWLED ON, AND SUDDENLY HEARD VOICES AHEAD OF ME. PERHAPS I WAS ALREADY AT THE ENEMY'S LINE. I WAS CONFUSED. I HAD TO CRAWL INTO A HOLE UNTIL MY HEAD CLEARED.

I SAW THE SENSELESSNESS OF MY FEAR, BUT THEN A NEW CONFUSION OVERTOOK ME. I HAD LOST ALL SENSE OF DIRECTION! I HEARD FEET TRODDING, BUT WHETHER OURS OR THE ENEMY'S I COULD NOT TELL. I GRASPED MY DAGGER AND LAY WAITING... DEATH TO ANYONE WHO ENTERED MY SHELL HOLE!

AND THEN IT HAPPENED...

THE BODY CONVULSED AND BECAME LIMP. WHEN I RECOVERED MYSELF, MY HAND WAS STICKY AND WET...

THE MAN STILL LIVED. I KNEW I SHOULD FINISH THE JOB, BUT I COULDN'T. I CRAWLED TO THE FARTHEST SIDE OF THE HOLE AND LISTENED TO THE DYING GURGLE IN HIS THROAT...

I FELT PANIC. I HAD TO GET AWAY, BUT IT WAS SUICIDE TO TRY. THE SHELLING AND FIRING WAS MUCH TOO HEAVY.

THROUGHOUT THE NIGHT, THE GURGLING CONTINUED. I TRIED TO STOP MY EARS, BUT IT WAS NO USE. I FOUND MYSELF SAYING OVER AND OVER THAT HE MUST NOT DIE. IN THE MORNING, I GOT HIM WATER AND BANDAGED HIS WOUNDS...

I WANT TO HELP YOU, COMRADE. I WANT TO HELP YOU!

HOW SLOWLY THE MAN DIED. BUT NOW HE WAS DEAD AND I SAT WITH HIS WALLET IN MY HANDS. I HAD KILLED A GÉRARD DUVAL, A PRINTER. I FELT I MUST MAKE AMENDS TO HIS WIFE, TO HIS CHILDREN. I SWORE THAT WHEN THIS WAS OVER, I WOULD SPEND THE REST OF MY LIFE LOOKING AFTER HIS FAMILY.

THE DAY PASSED AGAIN LIKE AN ETERNITY. THEN CAME TWILIGHT AND FINALLY, DARKNESS ONCE MORE. THE FRONT WAS QUIET. IF I COULD ONLY FIND MY WAY BACK TO MY LINES, I WOULD KEEP EVERY PROMISE.

I INCHED MY WAY ALONG, SLOWLY... SLOWLY. BY THE LIGHT OF A ROCKET, I SAW MOVEMENT NEAR THE WIRE. I RECOGNISED OUR HELMETS. I CALLED OUT...

PAUL! PAUL!

ARE YOU WOUNDED? WE HAVE A STRETCHER!

NO... NO...

I DID NOT MENTION THE DEAD PRINTER THAT NIGHT. BUT BY THE NEXT MORNING, I COULD KEEP IT NO LONGER...

KAT... OUT THERE... I KILLED A MAN! I WATCHED HIM DIE! FOR A NIGHT AND A DAY I WATCHED HIM DIE! I MUST MAKE AMENDS TO HIS FAMILY...

YOU CAN'T DO ANYTHING ABOUT IT. LOOK OVER THERE.

YOU SHOULD HAVE SEEN THAT LAST ONE LEAP IN THE AIR! I'VE KILLED THREE ALREADY!

I WOULD NOT DO IT.

DON'T LOSE ANY MORE SLEEP OVER IT. AFTER ALL, WAR IS WAR.

SOMETIME LATER, WE HAD A GOOD JOB; WE WERE TO GUARD A VILLAGE THAT HAD BEEN ABANDONED. WE WERE TO PROVISION OURSELVES FROM THE SUPPLY DUMP.

WE ARE JUST THE RIGHT MEN FOR THE JOB.

WE SELECTED A REINFORCED CONCRETE CELLAR AS A DUGOUT AND DEVELOPED IMMENSE INDUSTRY.

WHEN WE GET THROUGH HERE, WE'LL SEE IF WE CAN FIND A HEN COOP, AND PERHAPS SOME EGGS.

WE HAD NOT GONE FAR IN OUR SEARCH, WHEN WE CAME UPON...

LOOK, PAUL, A STOVE, WITH A WHOLE CHIMNEY! IF WE CAN FIND ANY MEAT, WE CAN COOK IT HERE!

OUR SEARCH REWARDED US WELL. WE HAD NETTED TWO SUCKLING PIGS, WHICH KAT HAD DRESSED, WHILE TJADEN HAD FOUND A GARDEN WITH POTATOES AND CARROTS...

HOW'S THAT FIRE COMING, PAUL?

IT COULDN'T BE BETTER. BRING ON THE ROAST!

THINGS WERE GOING FINE, BUT ENEMY OBSERVATION BALLOONS SPOTTED THE SMOKE FROM OUR CHIMNEY...

THIS WOULD BE A PIECE OF LUCK, TO BE BLOWN APART BEFORE WE HAVE A CHANCE TO ENJOY THIS MEAL!

I'M MAKING A DIVE FOR IT!

WE DASHED FROM THE "COOK-HOUSE" TO THE CELLAR AMID SHELLS AND EXPLOSIONS. KAT AND KROPP CARRIED THE MASTERPIECE, TJADEN THE CARROTS, MÜLLER THE POTATOES, WHILE I FOLLOWED UP WITH A DISH OF PANCAKES...

I THINK WE'RE GOING TO MAKE IT!

ABOUT TWO O'CLOCK WE STARTED THE MEAL. BY TEN O'CLOCK, WE WERE ON COGNAC, RUM, COFFEE AND CIGARS FROM THE OFFICERS' SUPPLY STORES...

WAIT, YOU! LISTEN!

LOOK WHAT IT IS! A KITTEN!

I WONDERED WHY I BROUGHT THIS PARROT CAGE ALONG. WE'LL FEED THE CAT AND LET IT SLEEP IN THIS.

ALMOST A FORTNIGHT PASSED IN EATING, DRINKING, RELAXING. NO ONE ROSE EARLY...

ALBERT, MY GOOD MAN, YOU MAY BRING THE CAVIAR AND COFFEE.

AND WHILE YOU'RE ABOUT IT, ALBERT, DRAW MY BATH!

ONE MOMENT, GENTLEMEN! TJADEN IS GOING TO DO MY MANICURE!

THE PALMY DAYS WERE OVER. WE WERE SENT OUT TO EVACUATE A VILLAGE. WE MET THE INHABITANTS ALREADY LEAVING, THEIR FACES FULL OF GRIEF, DESPAIR, RESIGNATION...

AT LEAST WE ARE QUITE SAFE. THE FRENCH DO NOT FIRE ON TOWNS IN WHICH THERE ARE INHABITANTS.

I SPOKE TOO SOON!

WE HAVE TO GET OUT OF HERE! ARE YOU OKAY?

I THINK IT GOT ME IN THE KNEE!

WE CRAWLED TO THE TOP OF THE DITCH. I HAILED A PASSING AMBULANCE WAGON...

HELP! WOUNDED!

AT THE DRESSING-STATION...

I DIDN'T REALISE I WAS WOUNDED, TOO. IT LOOKS LIKE WE'RE BOTH GETTING A VACATION!

I DON'T KNOW. MY LEG IS BAD. I'VE MADE UP MY MIND. I WON'T LIVE TO BE A CRIPPLE, PAUL!

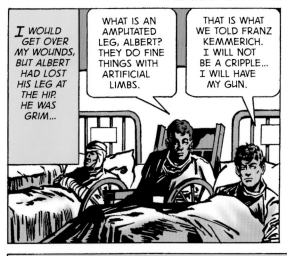

I WOULD GET OVER MY WOUNDS, BUT ALBERT HAD LOST HIS LEG AT THE HIP. HE WAS GRIM...

WHAT IS AN AMPUTATED LEG, ALBERT? THEY DO FINE THINGS WITH ARTIFICIAL LIMBS.

THAT IS WHAT WE TOLD FRANZ KEMMERICH. I WILL NOT BE A CRIPPLE... I WILL HAVE MY GUN.

I GOT CONVALESCENT LEAVE. PARTING FROM ALBERT KROPP WAS VERY HARD...

KEEP YOUR CHIN UP, ALBERT. I'LL BE SEEING YOU!

CALL IT GOOD-BYE, PAUL. WE WON'T EVER SEE EACH OTHER AGAIN.

I RECOVERED. OUR LIFE ALTERNATED BETWEEN THE BILLETS AND THE FRONT. WE HAD ALMOST GROWN ACCUSTOMED TO IT. WAR WAS A CAUSE OF DEATH, LIKE CANCER, OR TUBERCULOSIS. THE DEATHS ARE ONLY MORE FREQUENT, MORE VARIED, MORE TERRIBLE...

IT WAS WINTER WHEN I CAME BACK, AND FROZEN CLODS OF EARTH WERE AS DANGEROUS AS SHELL FRAGMENTS...

AND THE SPRING THAWS BROUGHT US MUD...

OUR ONLY COMFORT WAS HAVING LEARNED TO SLEEP, IN SPITE OF THE STEADY BOMBARDMENTS.

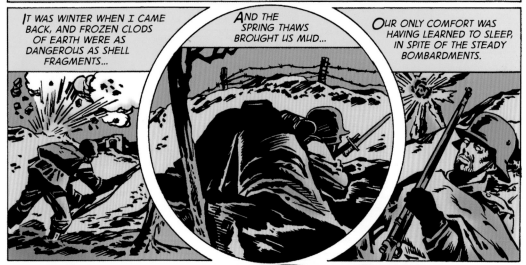

I SAW LIFE BREAKING DOWN AROUND ME. THERE WAS THE MAD STORY OF DETERING. WE WERE RETURNING FROM THE FRONT...

LOOK, FELLOWS! CHERRY BLOSSOMS!

THAT NIGHT...

HEY, HAS ANYONE SEEN DETERING?

HE WAS HERE A WHILE AGO.

HERE HE IS NOW... WITH A BUNCH OF CHERRY BLOSSOMS!

SAY, WHERE ARE YOU GOING, DETERING, TO A WEDDING?

I AWOKE IN THE NIGHT. DETERING WAS PULLING ON HIS BOOTS.

DON'T DO ANYTHING FOOLISH, DETERING.

ME? IT'S MERELY THAT I CAN'T SLEEP...

WHAT DID YOU PICK THE CHERRY BRANCHES FOR?

IT'S NOTHING. I HAVE A BIG ORCHARD OF CHERRY TREES AT HOME. IT IS JUST THE TIME.

THE NEXT MORNING...

ONE...

THREE...

FOUR...

WHERE IS NUMBER TWO? WHERE IS DETERING?

A WEEK LATER, WE LEARNED OF DETERING. THE MILITARY POLICE HAD STOPPED HIM. ANYONE MIGHT HAVE KNOWN THAT HIS FLIGHT WAS ONLY HOMESICKNESS AND A MOMENTARY ABERRATION OF THE MIND. BUT WHAT DOES A COURT-MARTIAL HUNDREDS OF MILES BEHIND THE FRONT LINES KNOW ABOUT IT? WE HEARD NOTHING MORE OF DETERING.

SOMETIMES, WAR MADNESS BROKE OUT IN OTHER WAYS. THERE WAS THE CASE OF BERGER...

LISTEN! A WOUNDED MESSENGER DOG. I'M GOING TO SAVE HIM!

DON'T BE A FOOL! THE MACHINE-GUN FIRE IS LIKE A SWARM OF MOSQUITOES.

ONE RECOGNISED THE MADNESS. BERGER, WHO MEANT TO HELP THE DOG, WAS BADLY WOUNDED... AND ONE OF THE FELLOWS HELPING BERGER GOT A BULLET IN THE CHEEK...

MÜLLER WAS DEAD. SOMEONE SHOT HIM POINT BLANK WITH A VERY LIGHT IN THE STOMACH. HE LIVED FOR HALF AN HOUR, CONSCIOUS AND IN TERRIBLE PAIN. BEFORE HE DIED...

WE WERE ABLE TO BURY MÜLLER. HE WAS NOT LIKELY TO REMAIN UNDISTURBED FOR LONG, FOR OUR LINES WERE FALLING BACK. NEVERTHELESS, IT WAS COMFORTING...

PAUL... YOU... YOU GET KEMMERICH'S BOOTS... NOW.

ASHES TO ASHES... DUST TO DUST...

LEER GOT IT IN THE HIP. HE GROANED AS HE SUPPORTED HIMSELF BUT HE BLED QUICKLY. NO ONE COULD HELP HIM. LIKE AN EMPTY TUBE, AFTER A COUPLE OF MINUTES, HE COLLAPSED. WHAT USE THAT HE WAS SUCH A GOOD MATHEMATICIAN IN SCHOOL?

THE MONTHS PASSED BY. THE SUMMER OF 1918 WAS THE MOST TERRIBLE. AMID RUMOURS OF PEACE, THE DYING WENT ON. WHY DO THEY NOT MAKE AN END? WHY? WHY?

41

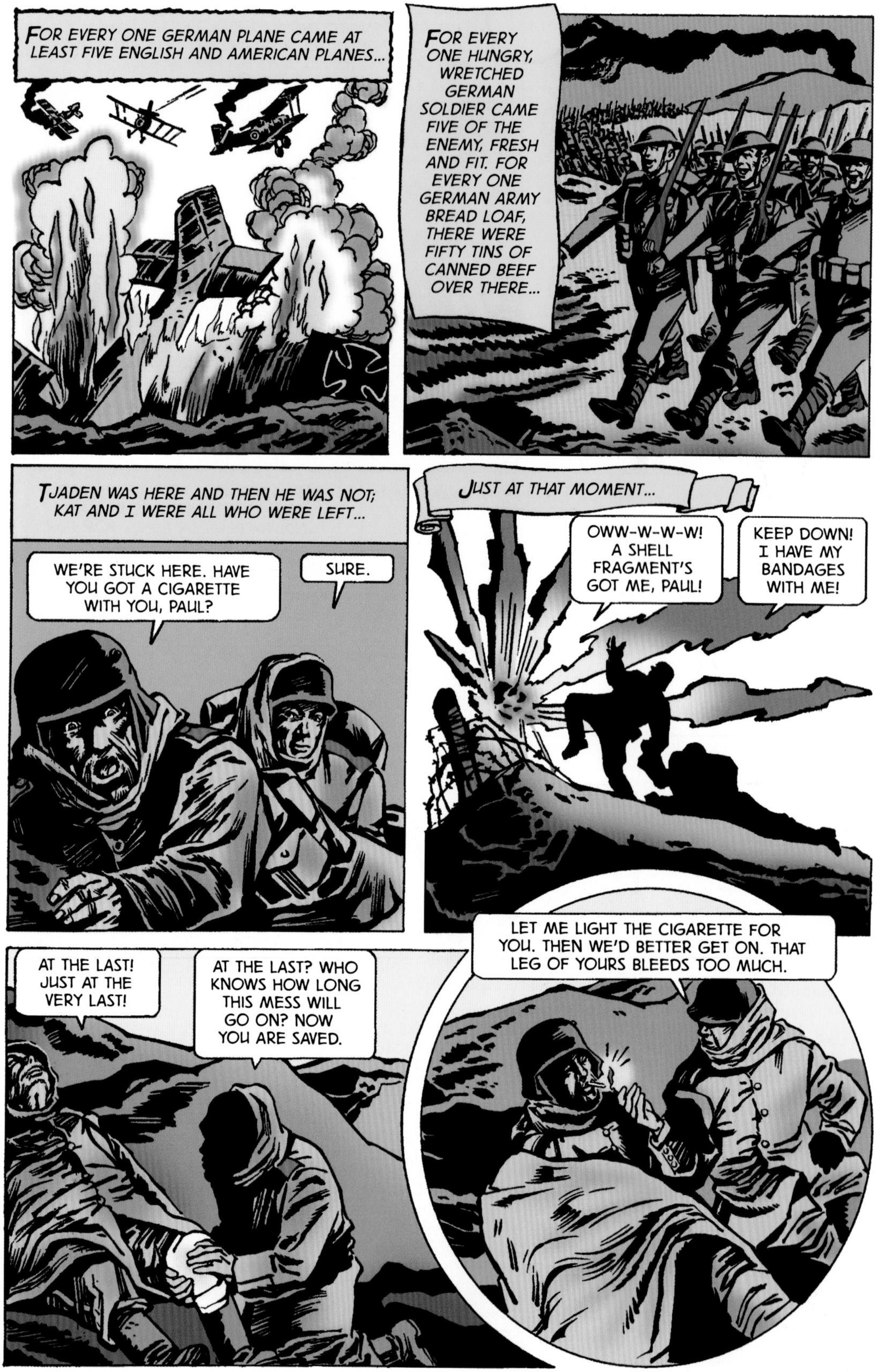
FOR EVERY ONE GERMAN PLANE CAME AT LEAST FIVE ENGLISH AND AMERICAN PLANES...
FOR EVERY ONE HUNGRY, WRETCHED GERMAN SOLDIER CAME FIVE OF THE ENEMY, FRESH AND FIT. FOR EVERY ONE GERMAN ARMY BREAD LOAF, THERE WERE FIFTY TINS OF CANNED BEEF OVER THERE...
TJADEN WAS HERE AND THEN HE WAS NOT; KAT AND I WERE ALL WHO WERE LEFT...
WE'RE STUCK HERE. HAVE YOU GOT A CIGARETTE WITH YOU, PAUL?
SURE.
JUST AT THAT MOMENT...
OWW-W-W-W! A SHELL FRAGMENT'S GOT ME, PAUL!
KEEP DOWN! I HAVE MY BANDAGES WITH ME!
AT THE LAST! JUST AT THE VERY LAST!
AT THE LAST? WHO KNOWS HOW LONG THIS MESS WILL GO ON? NOW YOU ARE SAVED.
LET ME LIGHT THE CIGARETTE FOR YOU. THEN WE'D BETTER GET ON. THAT LEG OF YOURS BLEEDS TOO MUCH.

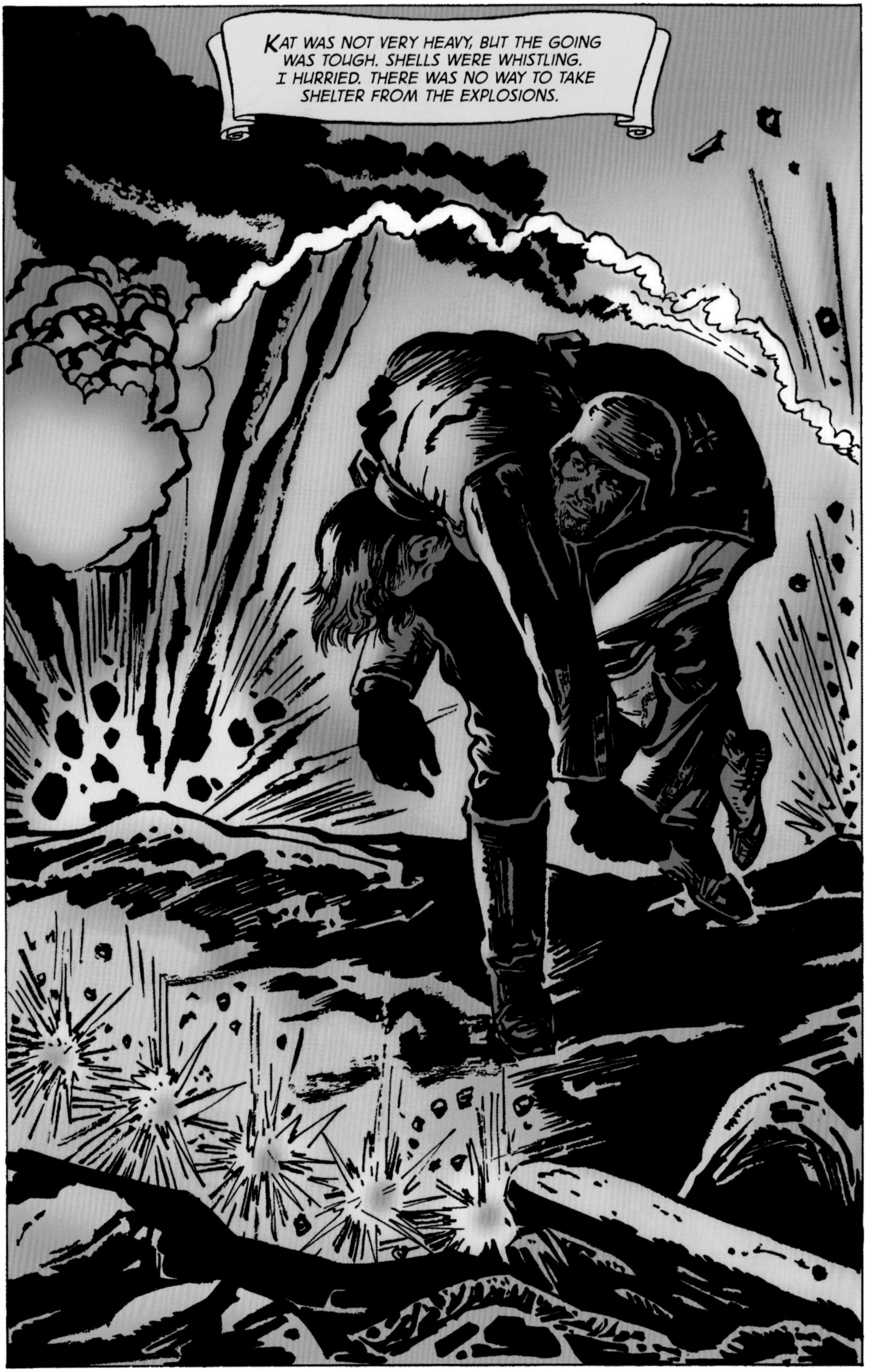
KAT WAS NOT VERY HEAVY, BUT THE GOING WAS TOUGH. SHELLS WERE WHISTLING. I HURRIED. THERE WAS NO WAY TO TAKE SHELTER FROM THE EXPLOSIONS.

KAT'S LEG DRIPPED BLOOD TO THE GROUND. I DARED NOT WAIT FOR A STRETCHER. I STAGGERED ON, DOGGEDLY AND PITILESSLY, AND AT LAST REACHED THE DRESSING-STATION.

I HAD JUST STRENGTH ENOUGH TO KEEP FROM INJURING KAT'S LEG AS I LET HIM DOWN.

ORDERLY! GIVE ME A HAND!

YOU MIGHT HAVE SAVED YOURSELF THAT TRIP.

WHAT DO YOU MEAN?

HE IS STONE DEAD.

I DON'T BELIEVE IT! HE WAS HIT IN THE SHIN!

HE IS DEAD.

HE'S ONLY FAINTED, I TELL YOU! I'LL RUB HIS TEMPLES!

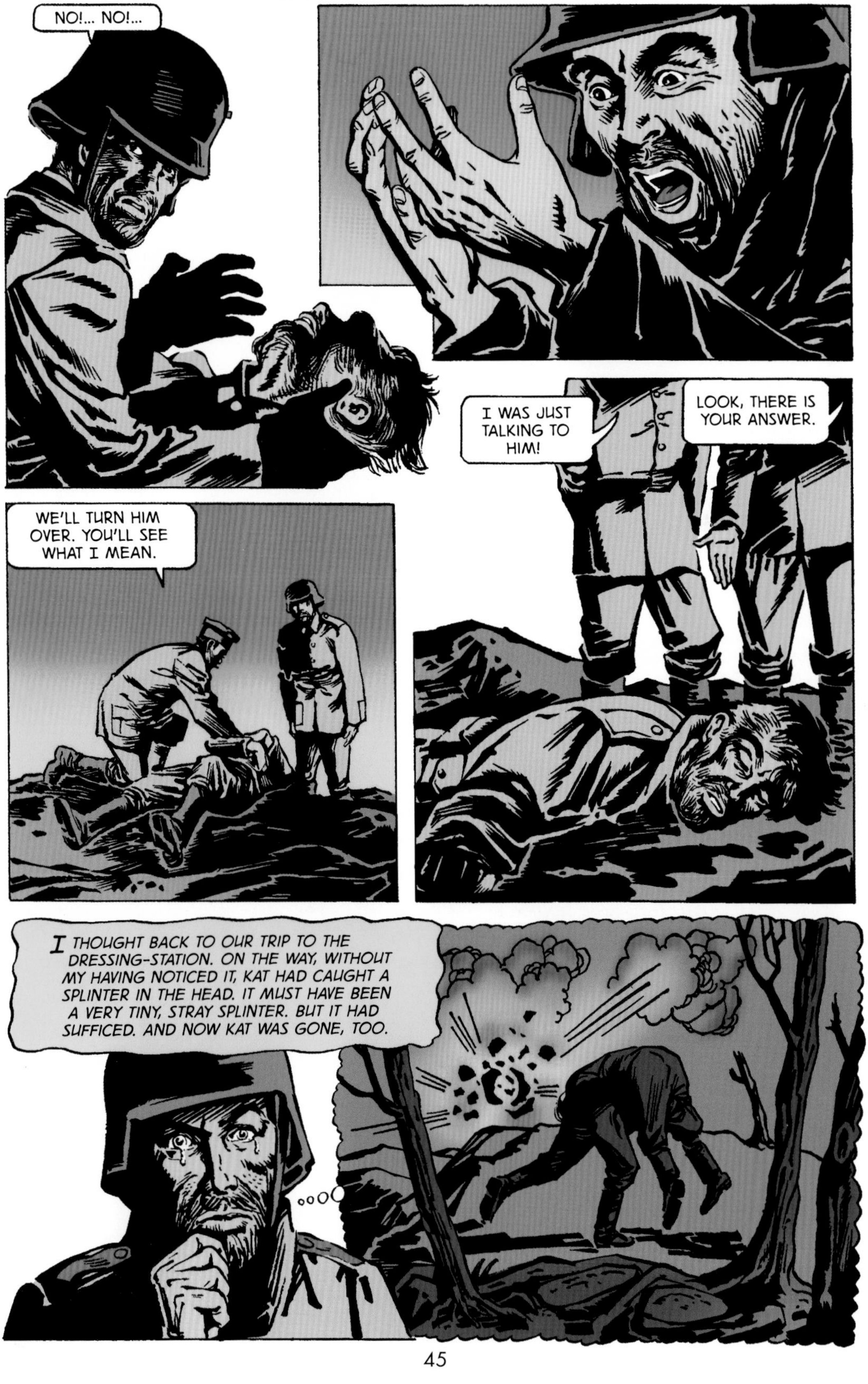
NO!... NO!...
I WAS JUST TALKING TO HIM!
LOOK, THERE IS YOUR ANSWER.
WE'LL TURN HIM OVER. YOU'LL SEE WHAT I MEAN.
I THOUGHT BACK TO OUR TRIP TO THE DRESSING-STATION. ON THE WAY, WITHOUT MY HAVING NOTICED IT, KAT HAD CAUGHT A SPLINTER IN THE HEAD. IT MUST HAVE BEEN A VERY TINY, STRAY SPLINTER. BUT IT HAD SUFFICED. AND NOW KAT WAS GONE, TOO.

WOULD YOU LIKE TO TAKE HIS PAY-BOOK AND HIS THINGS? ARE YOU RELATED?

YES... I WILL TAKE HIS THINGS. NO... WE ARE NOT RELATED... NOT RELATED...

COULD I WALK? HAD I FEET STILL? I RAISED MY EYES, LET THEM MOVE AROUND, TURNED MYSELF WITH THEM IN ONE CIRCLE. ALL WAS AS USUAL. ONLY MILITIAMAN STANISLAUS KATCZINSKY HAD DIED. THEN I KNEW NOTHING MORE.

IT IS AUTUMN. I HAVE FOURTEEN DAYS' REST, BECAUSE I HAVE SWALLOWED A BIT OF GAS. THE ARMISTICE IS COMING SOON. I BELIEVE IT NOW. I SIT THE WHOLE DAY LONG IN THE SUN, AND DREAM OF HOME. HERE MY THOUGHTS STOP.

I AM THE LAST OF US. THE WAY LEADS BACK INTO BATTLE. LET THE MONTHS AND THE YEARS COME. THEY CAN BRING ME NOTHING MORE. I AM SO ALONE, AND SO WITHOUT HOPE THAT I CAN CONFRONT THEM WITHOUT FEAR.

"THUS ENDS PAUL BÄUMER'S OWN STORY.

"PAUL BÄUMER FELL IN OCTOBER, 1918, ON A DAY THAT WAS SO QUIET AND STILL ON THE WHOLE FRONT, THAT THE ARMY REPORT CONFINED ITSELF TO THE SINGLE SENTENCE: ALL QUIET ON THE WESTERN FRONT.

"TURNING HIM OVER, ONE SAW THAT HE COULD NOT HAVE SUFFERED LONG. HIS FACE HAD AN EXPRESSION OF CALM, AS THOUGH ALMOST GLAD THE END HAD COME."

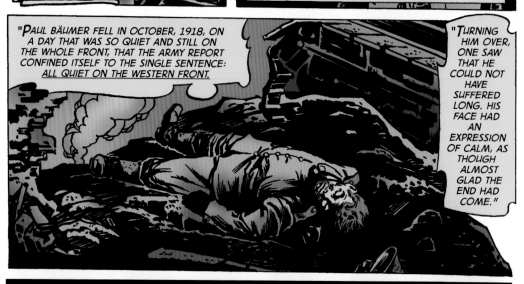

NOW THAT YOU HAVE READ THE CLASSICS ILLUSTRATED EDITION, WHY NOT GO ON TO READ THE ORIGINAL VERSION TO GET THE FULL ENJOYMENT OF THIS CLASSIC WORK?

Background

All Quiet on the Western Front is a disturbing look at war from the perspective of the average German foot soldier. Conspicuously absent from the book are generals, statesmen, or rulers of any kind. Names common to German military history of the period - von Moltke, von Ludendorff, von Falkenhayn - don't appear here; Hindenburg is mentioned once but never appears in the story; Kaiser Wilhelm II himself appears in a cameo role, and is then quickly dismissed. More importantly, the decisions made by these figures, even the cause of conflict itself, are never mentioned. Specific geographic locations aren't given, and the goals of the war are undetermined for both combatants and readers. The reader only knows the setting is somewhere along the Western Front. This indeterminate setting allows Remarque to put his fighting men of the trenches centre stage. *All Quiet* is their story, a tale of their agony and of their disillusionment. It is a story of "young innocents" compelled to risk life and limb, unmindful of the events that created the war.

World War I, the Great War, began with the assassination of Archduke Franz Ferdinand, heir to the Austro-Hungarian throne, by a Serbian nationalist, on June 28th, 1914, in the Bosnian capital of Sarajevo. But while the archduke's death was the spark which plunged the world into war, Europe at the time was a powder keg just waiting for the spark to fly. For decades, the rulers of Europe had competed for new markets, expanded borders, and colonial possessions in South America, Asia and Africa. As competitors, these nations - and their monarchs - maintained large armies and naval forces which provided a healthy profit for arms makers during times of conflict. At a time when the rivalries and conflicts among the monarchs were growing, they also faced the threat of emerging nationalism in the Balkans, the Middle East, and Africa: subjected peoples were ready to throw off the shackles of colonialism and seek nationhood. When the Archduke was killed, nation after nation, seized with fear that war was inevitable, made alliances to safeguard their borders - and possessions. Germany, Austria-Hungary, the Ottoman Empire (Turkey), and Bulgaria became known as the Central Powers, while Great Britain, France, Russia, Italy and, in 1917, the United States, became known as the Allies.

We tend to think of WWI as a European war, but in fact it was fought in Africa, Asia, and the Middle East as well. In Europe, the Eastern and Western Fronts divided the continent into a battleground larger than any since the Thirty Years War (1618-1648). It was fought in the deserts of the Middle East, where Arab tribesmen rebelled against their Turkish rulers of nearly 500 years, and in Africa where native colonials fought for their European masters. The worst bloodletting witnessed up to that time, the Great War (1914-1918) claimed some nine million military lives, with nearly thirty million more wounded, captured, or missing in action. And there were something like thirty million civilian casualties. The devastation of the Great War was brought on in large part due to new weapons technology: the introduction of the tank unleashed firepower and provided cover for advancing infantry. The German U-Boat, or submarine, made water travel treacherous for military and passenger vessels. The flamethrower scorched men and earth. Zeppelins, large dirigibles invented by the Germans, dropped death from the skies and served as observation sentinels. The aeroplane, made famous by daredevil flying aces, duelled in the sky and strafed infantrymen and civilians alike. Chemical warfare, first used systematically by the Germans at Ypres, Belgium, on April 25th, 1915, discharged cylinders of chlorine gas, which affected the lungs and **Cont'd** caused death by asphyxia with prolonged exposure; gas also burned and blistered the skin. On that day, advancing French troops recoiled, broke ranks, and retreated in panic clutching their throats. Finally, improved heavy artillery could wipe out columns of men, trenches, even towns - all from a distance.

Of all the war theatres, the Western Front was the most important; thus, it amassed the greatest number of troops per mile, and maintained the most elaborate fortifications. From the English Channel to the Swiss border was an almost continuous network of trenches; stretched in between opposing trenches was a deadly no-man's-land where some of the fiercest fighting and most grotesque forms of death waited. The trenches of western Europe provide the setting for *All Quiet on the Western Front*.

Trench warfare was not new to modern fighting, and it was used extensively in the First World War. Construction of trenches was complex: both machines and hand tools were used to dig trenches; timber was necessary to support them; pumps and pumping were necessary for drainage; duckboards for flooring; concrete to fortify them; countless miles of barbed wire to protect them; sandbags to crown and plug them; and telephone cable to connect them.

Movement between trenches was hindered by mud, water and other obstacles. Transportation of supplies, primarily done by draught horses, was tedious as well as dangerous. Dampness, rats, vermin and cold were common sources of discomfort. At some points along the Western Front, the subsoil water lay so close to the surface that trenches filled up as fast as they were dug; only frost brought a measure of relief. In the trenches, according to the English poet Robert Graves, who served there, ordinary foot soldiers "endured for four years perhaps the most sustained misery in recorded history." Graves's first-hand war memoir, *Goodbye to All That*, is remarkably like *All Quiet* in many ways; life in the trenches, he claimed, promoted an outlook that was very different from civilian beliefs. Patriotism was "sentiment fit only for civilians," claimed Graves. Similarly, Remarque's Paul Bäumer notes that "The Front is a cage," where "distinction, breeding, education... are blotted out." He continues, "We can hardly control ourselves when our hunted glance lights on the form of some other man. We are insensible, dead men, who through some trick, some dreadful magic, are still able to run and to kill." Bäumer describes the men at the Front as those who are "crude and sorrowful" and "condemned." Nothing mattered at the Front except the drive for survival.

In spite of bitter fighting on the Western Front, two years of almost constant battle produced nothing more than a military impasse in a deadly war of attrition. The history of the Western Front was a series of attacks and counter-attacks. On August 3rd, 1914, Germany invaded neutral Belgium in order to strike at France. By September 2nd, 1914, the Allies were hard-pressed at the Seine, the Marne, and Meuse above Verdun. Ten days later, the Allies assumed the offensive on the Aisne. For roughly the next two years, trench warfare on the Western Front claimed millions of casualties, with no clear victory in sight. From one end of the continent to the other, claims historian David M. Kennedy, the military stand-off made "a charnel house of Europe."

On February 21st, 1916, the Germans renewed their attack on Verdun, and by early June, Verdun fell. The following month the Allies attacked the Germans at the Somme; by mid-July, 1917, the French had retaken Verdun. On March 21st, 1918, the massive German offensive from Arras to La Fere came within fifty miles of Allied ***Cont'd*** troops in France. On April 4th, 1918, the Germans advanced near Amiens, but the British and French lines held. The United States' entry into the war in April of 1918 helped bring victory to the Allies: on May 28th, 1918, American troops, in their first important offensive, captured Cantigny. On June 11th, 1918, French and American troops drove into Bellou Wood, made gains at Château-Thierry, and crossed the Marne. On July 18th, 1918, the great Allied drive had begun, and by September, they had driven the Germans eastward. Elsewhere, the Central Powers were demoralised and in retreat as well. As Paul Bäumer concludes towards the end of All Quiet, "Our artillery is fired out, it has too few shells and the barrels are so worn that they shoot uncertainly, and scatter so widely as even to fall on ourselves. We have too few horses. Our fresh troops are anaemic boys in need of rest, who cannot carry a pack, but merely know how to die. By thousands." On November 9th, 1918, the Kaiser abdicated; the Armistice was signed two days later. The slaughter on the Western Front had finally come to an end.

The defeat put further strain upon Germany after the war. Allied leaders demanded huge reparations from the defeated Central Powers, with Germany assuming the lion's share. Limitations were set upon the German military. Germany was stripped of its African colonies, and made to assume guilt for the war itself. This last - war guilt - proved most difficult for Germany to swallow; in 1933, Adolf Hitler began to rally the German people to avenge this insult, and, in 1939, plunged the world into war again.

Today, much of what had been the Western Front is quiet, picturesque and pastoral. Cattle graze, vineyards flourish, wooded hills with sparkling streams make up much of the area that between 1914 and 1918 was a maelstrom of death. Museums and cemeteries keep alive the memory and importance of the Western Front. Rusted barbed wire posts and decaying gun turrets dot the landscape, as do bright red signs, warnings indicating unexploded hardware beneath the quiet surface.

Themes

Disillusionment

The theme of disillusionment is played out many times in All Quiet on the Western Front. Bäumer notes early in the story, "With our young awakened eyes we saw that the classical conception of the Fatherland held by our teachers resolved here into a renunciation of personality such as one would not ask of the meanest servant." German visions of past glories fade quickly and the call to sacrifice for the Fatherland rings hollow at the Front. The war has placed a heavy burden upon an entire generation. Kropp notes, "Two years of shells and bombs - a man won't peel that off as easy as a sock." He continues, "The war ruined us for everything." Bäumer concedes that they are not youth anymore. The recruits evade everyone and everything except their own fellowship. "The first bomb," claims Bäumer, "the explosion burst in our hearts. We are cut off from activity, from striving, from progress. We believe in such things no longer, we believe in the war." This does not mean that the recruits support the war, but that they have become dehumanised by the conflict, and captive to it. War is the only experience they can relate to. "We are forlorn like children," laments Paul Bäumer, "and experienced like old men, we are crude and sorrowful. I believe we are lost." He later adds, "I see how people's sights are set against one another. I see that the keenest brains of the world invent weapons and words to make it yet more refined and enduring." It does not take Bäumer and his classmates long to **Cont'd** recognise the motives of the profit-seekers, the politicians, and the generals who find the war "useful." They are no longer innocent youth, but hardened veterans, embittered and disillusioned.

Camaraderie

Early on, Remarque's sympathies become apparent: Paul Bäumer comes to prefer the company of his fellow soldiers to his family. The young recruits have come to rally behind each other for comfort, solace, and support. They seek each other out. The second company serves as a surrogate family for the young recruits. What they have been forced to endure, commit, and suffer has forced them to turn inward. They have come to understand the realities of war, and they have also come to realise the tremendous support that only their comrades can provide.

This camaraderie carries across military lines as well. The Russian prisoners of war, "silent and guiltless," are comrades-in-arms. They, too, are forced to endure the misery and savagery of the war. The French infantryman whom Bäumer must kill in the shell hole is also a comrade in the struggle. At one point, shortly after the Frenchman dies, Bäumer murmurs, "Comrade, today you, tomorrow me."

The young infantrymen share a sense of the tragic that is never mute in the novel, only violent and brutal. To insulate themselves from this brutality, the soldiers take refuge in each other's company.

Death

In novels about war, death is a constant theme. But death can be noble, heroic, and chivalrous. Dying in the quest for some great cause is commonplace in the annals of history and mythology. Any sense of heroic death in *All Quiet*, however, is entirely missing. The young recruits are not even sure what they are fighting and dying for. Death in *All Quiet* is grotesque. Deaths are caused by gas attacks. Men are discovered with noses cut off and eyes poked out and stuffed with sawdust so they slowly suffocate in the trenches. In one scene, Bäumer's company comes upon the upper torso of a dead soldier in a tree, wearing only its helmet. The gurgles of the dying are haunting. Bloated corpses that hiss and belch in death are littered about. In a graveyard battle scene, the young volunteers seek shelter in coffins that have been unearthed by heavy artillery shelling. They scramble to throw out the bodies of the dead and crawl in to take their places. There is no chivalry at the Western Front, only death, grotesque death.

Anti-War

Remarque's determination to strip warfare of its glory and any sense of regeneration defines *All Quiet* as an anti-war novel. In an interview late in his life, Remarque proclaimed that he was always a pacifist. The book reveals no redeeming qualities in war. *All Quiet*'s characters demonstrate bravery; they think and speak of love and opportunity, but they are resigned to the fact that they now exist, and will probably die, in the human wasteland called the Front. Their spirits and sensibilities have been so bruised that they cannot even envision a future. The actions of Kantorek, the brow-beating school-master, and Himmelstoss, the mean-spirited Prussian drillmaster, violate twentieth century sensibilities. Both are adamantly pro-war, zealously nationalistic, belligerent, and downright disagreeable. Everything they personify is rejected by the youth. So, too, the parochial, autocratic, Teutonic militaristic code holds little appeal today for many readers sensitive to a more open and democratic global environment. The book's anti-war slant represents a departure from the German nationalist legacy.

Discussion Topics

1) Think of the new weapons technologies available in World War I. How do you think they affected the common foot soldiers like Paul Bäumer? Consider what you know of earlier wars. How do you think World War I was different?

2) By the end of *All Quiet on the Western Front*, almost every young man in the book is dead or maimed in some way - even Paul Bäumer, the main character. Why do you think Remarque did this?

3) When Paul Bäumer goes home, he finds it difficult to deal with his family, yet when he returns to the Front it's as if he's gone home again. Why can he relate better to his comrades at the Front than with his family?

4) Remarque omits mention of almost every major political or historical figure from the war. Why? What effect does this have on the story's viewpoint?

5) *All Quiet on the Western Front* is clearly pacifistic and anti-war. What other books do you know that have similar themes? How do their authors state or effect those themes?

6) What impact, if any, do you think a book like *All Quiet on the Western Front* might have had during later wars, such as the Korean War, the Vietnam War, or the Gulf Wars?

Key Timeline of WWI

1914: June 28th - Austro-Hungarian Archduke Franz Ferdinand is assassinated in Sarajevo by Gavrilo Princip.

July 5th - Kaiser Wilhelm II promises support for Austria in war against Serbia.

July 28th - Austria declares war on Serbia.

August 1st - 3rd - Germany declares war on Russia and France and invades Belgium.

August 4th - Britain declares war on Germany.

August 23rd - Germany invades France.

September 6th - The Battle of the Marne begins.

October 18th - First Battle of Ypres.

October - Trench warfare begins.

1915: April 25th - Allied troops land at Gallipoli.

May 7th - The *Lusitania* is sunk by a German U-boat.

May 23rd - Italy declares war on Germany and Austria.

December -The Allies begin evacuation of Gallipoli.

1916: February 21st - Battle of Verdun begins.

May 31st - Battle of Jutland.

July 1st - Battle of the Somme begins.

1917: April 6th - USA declares war on Germany.

July 31st - Third Battle of Ypres begins.

December 5th - Russia surrenders to Germany.

1918: July 15th - Second Battle of the Marne. German army begins to fall.

November 9th - Kaiser Wilhelm II abdicates.

November 11th - Armistice is signed between Germany and the allies. WWI ends.